HOTEL FOR DOGS™

The Guest Book

BY ALISON INCHES

BASED ON THE BOOK BY
LOIS DUNCAN

SCREENPLAY BY
JEFF LOWELL AND
BOB SCHOOLEY & MARK McCORKLE

★ MEMO ★

To: Staff
From: Andi
Re: Cooper

Keep Cooper out of Room 502!
(If he chews my vintage
dresses, he'll be on a h[u]
doggie time-out!)

Simon Spotlight
New York   London   Toronto   Sydney

Andi & Dave
4-ever!

Based on the movie *Hotel For Dogs*™

SIMON SPOTLIGHT

An imprint of Simon & Schuster Children's Publishing Division
1230 Avenue of the Americas, New York, New York 10020

Manufactured in the United States of America
10 9 8 7 6 5 4 3 2
ISBN-13: 978-1-4169-7570-0
ISBN-10: 1-4169-7570-5

ANDI

Hey, I'm Andi. Welcome to the Hotel For Dogs! We're a full-service dog boarding and adoption agency. We take all kinds of dogs: chewers, howlers, herders, lickers, fetchers, car chasers, sniffers. You name it, we got it.

Before we got here, the hotel was abandoned. Yup, totally empty, except for the two strays that lived here, Lenny and Georgia. Our dog, Friday, loved staying here with them, and since our foster family didn't allow dogs, it was the perfect solution.

But that was a long time ago! Today my brother, Bruce, and I have real parents, Bernie and Carol. They're awesome! Together we own and operate the Hotel For Dogs. Oh, and Friday works here too.

Come on in and meet our canine clientele, serve up some kibble, mop up some drool, and scoop some poop! Oh, and don't forget to sign our guest book when you're done reading!

xoxo, Andi

BRUCE

FRIDAY

BRUCE

It's me, Bruce. Wow—the Hotel For Dogs sure is a howling success! Before the hotel reopened, my sister, Andi, and I were stuck with the Scudders, and boy oh boy, did that stink! All we had was Friday—and each other. But then we found the hotel, and soon it became our mission to rescue stray dogs and find good homes for them—no dog left behind!

As for me, I like to invent stuff—machines, gadgets, you name it. That's what I do at the Hotel For Dogs—rig cool inventions for the dogs. They seem to like it, and I love to make the dogs happy. Incidentally, we can't get some of the dogs to leave even AFTER they're adopted. . . .

Catchya Later!
—Bruce

WHAT ARE YOUR DOG INVENTION IDEA...

HOTEL FOR DOGS' FAVORITE INVENTIONS:

Romeo was here!

The Pee Room Stroll-a-Coaster

self-feeding machine

Date   Guest   Resi...   Rm

FRIDAY

FOOD!

Photographs are yummy!

Hey, I'm Friday. I'm Top Dog around here! What's up? Everyone who comes to the hotel wants to hear the story of how I met Andi and Bruce—so here goes! Back when I was a homeless pup, I spent my time snooping for food scraps. Well, one day I sniffed out this amazing picnic. The picnickers were off playing Frisbee, and before you could say, "Gulp!" I scarfed down their dinner. I'm a bottomless pit, what can I say?

Typed by Andi

When the family spotted me, I tried to run for it, but I was too stuffed to move. Busted! Luckily Andi and Bruce felt sorry for me and adopted me as their own. They argued about what to name me all the way home. They picked Friday because Friday was family picnic day. I wasn't so sure about it at first, but it's definitely grown on me.

Your Top Dog —Friday

ABOUT Me:

Favorite Accessory:
Bone-Sweet-Bone pillow
Favorite Activity:
Eating, or looking for good eats
Favorite Trick:
Backing out of a leash and collar
Favorite Sound:
Can opener

Dislikes: The pound, Lois's lumpy stew, dog catcher's loop

My Special Quality: Smell-O-Vision

 Job: Hotel For Dogs Pack Leader

Bone Sweet Bone

Ain't too proud to beg!

Oops, I think I got into some paint!

'All bark . . .

. . . and no bite.'

LENNY

WOOOF! Lenny here. I'm a BIG dog—big body, big bark—that scares some people. But what they don't know is that I also have a great big loving heart. Me and Georgia were the first ones to live here, back when this place was a dump. We used to whimper on cold nights. To make matters worse, Georgia snores like crazy—*Honk-shoo! Honk-shoo!*—all night long. As her best friend, I've learned to look past it.

One thing I need is a room with a view, or I'll go bonkers. Bruce rigged a machine that shines pretty views on the walls. It's heaven. Sometimes when the moon is on, I howl. It gets the other dogs going, if ya know what I mean. *A-a-a-a O-o-o-o-o-o-o!*
Big wags,
Lenny

GEORGIA

Yap! Yap! I'm Georgia. *Yip! Yap!* I go full-tilt boogie all the time. Lenny is my bestest—yip, yap—buddy in the whole world. *Yap! Yap!* He sticks up for me and stuff. *Yip! Yip!* By the way, I love to play fetch! *Yap! Yap!* Bruce made me an automatic fetching machine. Now I can play fetch all the time. I'm so fast! *Yip! Yip!* I'm like a boomerang! You know—back and forth, back and forth? It never gets old. *Yip! Yip!* It's a blast! Hey, Len, am I talking too much here?

MY FAVORITE
THINGS TO FETCH:

Dirty socks   Silverware
Frisbee   Tennis ball   Stuffed skunk
Cloth dinner napkins

DOES NOT
RESPOND TO
"GEORGE."

COOPER

My top 10. chew toys

1. Expensive shoes
2. Mail order—any kind
3. Work boots
4. Stuffed animals
5. Plastic pork chops
6. Pillows
7. Curtains
8. Bathing suits
9. Action figures
10. Rubber chickens

Recycling Engineer!

Yo, I'm Cooper. Some of my friends call me "Thrasher" and "Goat"—that's because I LOVE TO CHEW! See these chompers? If this hotel held a shoe-chewing contest, I would be the CHOMP-ion! Not to brag, but I've already chewed my way to the top of this place. I'm head of the Hotel For Dogs recycling program. That's right, I shred old newspapers. The funnies are particularly tasty.

Chew on! —Cooper

Move along, little doggies! Move along! Shep's the name, herding's my game! I keep the Hotel For Dogs in ship shape with my exceptional herding skills. Feel a little nip at your heels? Not to worry. It's just me. It means: Hop to it—we haven't got all day! These are strictly love nips—no one's going to get hurt as long as they just keep moving.

SHEP

BAAAAAA!

FAVORITE ROOM: HERDING ROOM

PUPPY 911

SHEP NANNIES FOR PUPS!
NO ONE STRAYS FROM THE LITTER!
RECOMMENDATIONS UPON REQUEST.

Romeo

PUPPY LOVE!

Who's your doggie?

Call me!

Dog Lover!

Furry Friends!

Puppy Love!

Ah, fair hotel guests! 'Tis I, Romeo—a dog that hath found true love. I fetcheth not newspapers, but chaseth only the lovely Juliet. Ah, fair Juliet! I will never stray from thee. If thou flee-est to the rooftop, I will find you there. If thou makest thy bed in an alleyway, behold, I will sleep with thee there. Oh, Juliet! Juliet! I love the way your groomed toenails clicketh along the halls and the way you flicketh your curly, snow white hair when you run hither and yon. Thou has never known such true love as Juliet!

P. S. Hark! Is that a choir of angels I hear?

ROMEO & JULIET'S TOP FIVE ROMANTICAL SPOTS

The Snuggle Room

The Rooftop Garden   Juliet's Balcony

The Dining Room

The Movie Room

Furry friends!

After!

JULIET

Before . . .

Well, howdy there! I'm Juliet. When I came to the Hotel For Dogs, I was a total wreck. Street life had matted and soiled my fur. Mark found me and won my trust with a banana. Ooo, I just love bananas!

May we have a little privacy?

Puppy Love!

At the Hotel For Dogs Puppy Spa, Heather pampered and primped me with a complete makeover—wash, massage, cut, fluff, and blow-dry. On my way out of the spa I bumped into Romeo. Oh, Romeo! Where for art thou? Be my sworn love, for how I pant to sit on the rooftop and gaze into your eyes!

Dog Lover!

Romeo & Juliet True Love

Romeo's Top Five Pick-up Lines:

1. Dost thou come here often?
2. Gee, your fur smells terrific!
3. Bow-wow WOW!
4. Is that the sun coming up, or did you just light up my world?
5. Woof! You look like my future wife!

HEATHER

Hey, I'm Heather, former pet-store worker. When Andi and Bruce discovered the Hotel For Dogs, Dave and I jumped at the chance to help out. What a dream come true for an animal lover like me! Now that the hotel is officially open, I welcome visitors and new dogs. Henry works with me on security. He can sniff out a bad dog owner with one good whiff! Come see us soon!

Heather

P.S. One of my special talents is doggie makeovers. No appointment necessary.

Date   Guest

Yo, what's up? It's Mark. I used to work at the grocery store down the street. One day I spied dogs and kids at the old hotel, so I checked it out. Back then the hotel was a secret operation. When I said I wanted to help, Andi and Bruce gave me Poop Duty. I regretted it for a bit, but now I help rescue strays. I load my trusty trench coat with doggie treats and lure them to safety. I hope to lure in Heather, too. (What a cutie!)

See ya, Mark

MARK

"HERE, BOY!"

DAVE

THE DOGMOBILE!

Hi, I'm Dave. I rescue strays in the trusty Dogmobile. Once I even rescued Andi when she was in trouble. Andi's the greatest. I've had my eye on that girl since the moment we met. Oh, uh, I didn't quite mean . . . well, uh, oh forget it. I gotta go now.

—Dave

HENRY

Rrrowff! I'm Henry. My first owner wanted me to be a vicious guard dog. But that's not for me. I'd much rather lick people and have my belly scratched than bully anyone. But don't get me wrong—if someone's in danger, I can be tough.

I owe everything to Bruce. He brought me to the Hotel For Dogs, and I love it here. Oh, and I have a great job as head of security. I check out the visitors and make sure they're all right. I give *this* place two paws up—way up!

—Henry

SCRATCH this cutie Anytime!

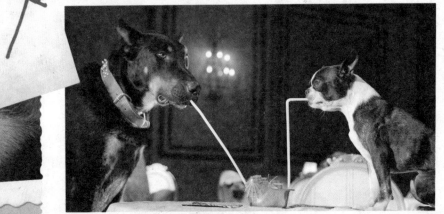

Me And my pAL

ADOPTED

VIOLA

SeBASTIAN

Arf! I'm Viola! Arf! Arf! And I'm Sebastian. We've lived on the streets since we were puppies, and no matter what, we stick together. One time we got chased by the Animal Control Officers and we wound up at the pound, but at least we were together.

CENTRAL CITY ANIMAL CONTROL

Not fun.

At the Hotel For Dogs, we still do everything together—bark at the doors in the Knocking Room, run on the treadmills. We even share the same bed. But guess what? Today we're being adopted! We'll sure miss the Hotel For Dogs. If you're new to the hotel, all we can say is, you're gonna love it!

Yours truly,
Viola & Sebastian

Lois

Yeah, this is Lois, and I just have to say that it's going to take a lot of years for Andi and Bruce to make up for all the valuable stuff they stole from us while we were their foster parents. We gave those kids some of the best years of our lives. Kids, if you're reading this, I want you to know you still owe us. But hey, you did get us a pretty cool gig here at the hotel. What really rocks is that we have a great audience every night. Give it up for the Carl Scudder Experience nightly at seven o'clock sharp!

Lois

"Stray Dog Strut"

TONIGHT AT 7 P.M.
THE CARL SCUDDER EXPERIENCE
COME HEAR OUR HIT SONGS!
"STRANDED BEACHED WHALE!" AND "STRAY DOG STRUT"

This is Carl of the Carl Scudder Experience. We're the featured entertainment at the Hotel For Dogs—our best gig yet. It's steady work, and the dogs really dig us. People told us to give up our rock 'n' roll dream and get real jobs. But we stuck to our dream, and all the years and all the tears have been worth it. Let's keep rockin' this house!

Carl

Carl

Hey, can someone spot me a buck?

BERNIE

ADOPTION APPROVED

It's Bernie here. I always knew Andi and Bruce were special—right from the beginning. And how I longed to find those kids the perfect foster family—I just can't believe it took me so long to realize what a good team we'd make. Don't get me wrong though, man, they are a couple of troublemakers! They almost cost me my job once or twice!

MEMO

TO: ANDI AND BRUCE

FROM: BERNIE AND CAROL

Re: Rooftop Garden BBQ at 6 p.m.

BYOD—Bring your own dog!

Things have been great since my wife and I adopted Andi and Bruce. Now we're a family. The Hotel For Dogs is our home, our family, and our livelihood. It's funny how things have a way of working out.

HOTEL
FOR DOGS

Adoption Center

FRICK

We're Frick and Frack.
We used to be pampered pugs.
We had silk pillow beds,
steak for dinner every night,
and daily romps in the park.
When our owner died, we
were left on the streets—cold,
lost, and hungry. The Hotel
For Dogs rescued us and
brought us in. We love it
here. We highly recommend
the Stroll-a-Coaster.

FRACK

*Achoo! It's me, Ginger. So my
old master's girlfriend sneezed
whenever she got near me.
She said I had to go. I didn't
understand it—I was so loyal!
Anyway, I wandered the streets
and finally wound up here. My
new master doesn't do much,
but he loves it when I fetch his
paper all day long! This place is
wonderful—maybe even better
than my old home.*

Another satisfied customer,

Ginger

GINGER

ADOPTED

MADISON

Personally, I don't care if I ever get adopted. I love the Hotel For Dogs. What's not to love? I have tons of friends, lots to do, and plenty to eat. This place is paws-itively amazing!

Yours, Maddie Girl

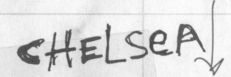

CHELSEA

Did you see a ball go by here? I just love to chase things, but sometimes they get away from me. Unfortunately, one time I did catch up with the ball and a car caught up with me, which is why my friends now call me "Tripod." But I figure I've still got one more leg than humans, so I'm still way faster than they are. Hey, someone just threw a Frisbee.

Gotta run!

Chelsea

Date	Guest	Comments	Rm.
5.2	GEORGIA	HAS Anyone seen A RED FRISBEE? PLEASE DROP it off At Room 105. THANKS!	105
☆	BRUCE	Found: One half-chewed red pump. See front desk.	
6.7	DAVE	Doggone it! Has anyone seen my Dogmobile keys?	83
6.23	SCOTTY	Mommy and I had a great time! Thanks, HFD!	326

Write your own comments! ↓